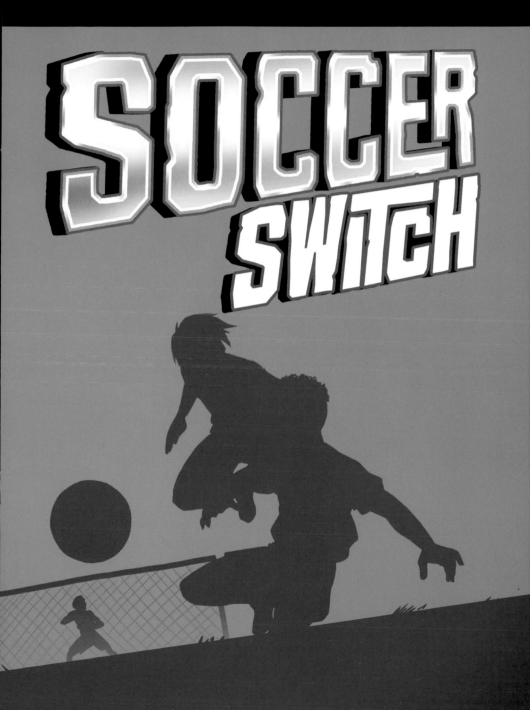

STONE ARCH BOOKS
a capstone imprint

JAKE MADDOX
GRAPHIC NOVELS

Jake Maddox Graphic Novels are published by
Stone Arch Books, a Capstone imprint
1710 Roe Crest Drive
North Mankato, Minnesota 56003

www.mycapstone.com

Library of Congress Cataloging-in-Publication Data
is available on the Library of Congress website.

ISBN: 978-1-4965-3699-0 (library binding)
ISBN: 978-1-4965-3703-4 (paperback)
ISBN: 978-1-4965-3719-5 (ebook PDF)

Summary: Andre Makuza is excited for
another championship season with his
middle school summer soccer team. But
a new coach is taking over, and his unusual
training methods have the team feeling frustrated.
Will the coach's oddball ways ever lead to victory,
or is the soccer switch too much for Andre and his
teammates to handle?

Editor: Abby Huff
Designer: Brann Garvey
Production: Gene Bentdahl

Printed in the United States of America.
042017   010473R

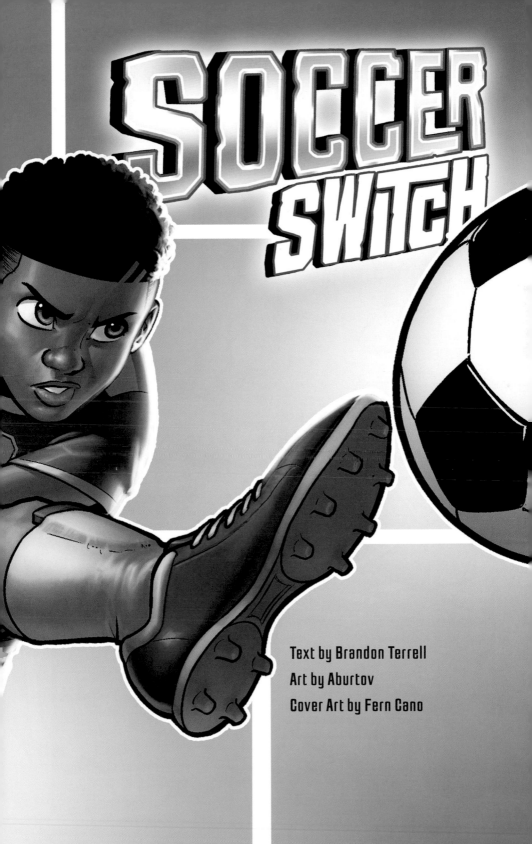

Text by Brandon Terrell

Art by Aburtov

Cover Art by Fern Cano

THE STARTING LINEUP

10

ANDRE MAKUZA

21

CULLIN HAWKE

16

HENRY YU

7

TAYE FOSTER

COACH BARNES

How I spent my summer!

Hi. My name is Andre Makuza, and this is the story about how I spent my summer vacation.

For as long as I can remember, I've loved soccer. Every summer, I play in a league with a bunch of friends.

It's awesome.

Here goes nothing.

"And 'nothing' was exactly what I saw."

"Not a single thing."

OK, let's run down the field. Stop on my command.

Run? You expect us to *run* in these?

Huff . . . huff . . .

Andre? Is that you?

I can't see where — *whoa!*

THUMP

Sorry.

34

"Even on the rare occasions when we *did* have a chance to score . . ."

". . . the Cyclones goalkeeper was a brick wall."

WHUMP

"The Cyclones, on the other hand . . ."

FWISH

FWISH

FWISH

BOBCATS 0
GUEST 5

"It was a tough start to the Bobcats' season."

"After I got home that night, after Coach Barnes had us dancing instead of playing soccer . . ."

"I started to understand Cullin's frustrations."

"I was as close to quitting as I'd ever been before."

"I almost called Cullin that second to tell him he was right about Coach Barnes."

"Instead, I made a promise to myself . . ."

I'll give it one more game.

"And oh man, what a game."

"We had a very special guest watching us play."

"Yeah, it was —"

Coach Winston?

Oh man, he's going to see us get crushed.

UGH. This is the worst thing in the world that could possibly happen.

43

Hard work, determination, and loyalty have always been the greatest virtues for a Bobcat.

You all displayed this today. Especially your striker . . .

. . . Andre.

He's a fine example of a team leader.

I *know.* Coach Winston knew who I was.

I was totally geeking out.

I spent my

"But then I spied someone in the crowd, and I wasn't listening to Coach Winston anymore."

"We had the following day off."

COMMUNITY POOL

"And what better way to spend a hot summer day than to —"

SPLOOSH

Nice cannonball, Andre!

WOOOSH

Ha! Whoa, dude. I gotta learn how to move my feet like that!

"Plus, Coach Barnes brought out the blindfolds again."

"This time, Cullin didn't trip over anything."

I can smell Andre's B.O.! He must be close!

Good! Use your other senses!

WHOOMP

"We took that goofy, excited energy right into our next game."

VISUAL QUESTIONS

1. Andre doesn't reply after Cullin and Taye say how upset they are about practice and the new coach. But with graphic novels, you can often figure out what a character is thinking through his facial expression. What does Andre's expression tell you? What might he be thinking?

2. Why are some panels completely black during the blindfold drill? How does not seeing anything help you understand what the players are experiencing?

3. Why is Cullin upset? Look back through the story and write down three reasons he's feeling frustrated.

4. Describe what's happening in this panel. Why is Andre shown four times in one panel? Talk about your answer.

5. What is Andre wearing around his neck? Were you surprised by the ending? In your own words, write a paragraph about how the team was able to turn their season around and come out champions.

ALL-STAR SOCCER MOVES

Ready to up your game? Soccer — or football, as it's known to most of the world — requires coordination, control, and speed. Read on to learn about advanced techniques that'll challenge your skills. Remember, practice is key to perfecting any new move!

CRUYFF TURN

Beat a defender with this classic turn. Put one foot to the side of the ball. Reach around the ball with your other foot. Stop the ball briefly with the inside of your foot. Pull the ball back. Turn and start dribbling in the other direction. First used by Dutch soccer player Johan Cruyff in the 1970s, this turn is still a popular dribbling skill.

RONALDO CHOP

Try out a signature move from famous Portuguese soccer pro Cristiano Ronaldo. As you're dribbling, take a small hop over the ball with both feet. Bring one foot down in front of the ball. Use the inside of your other foot to kick the ball as you land. Be sure to angle your foot at 45 degrees so you tap the ball forward. The sudden change in direction is perfect for throwing off a charging defender.

RAINBOW

Send the ball flying in an arc over your opponent. Use your dominant foot to roll the ball up the back of your other leg. Lean forward and quickly flick the ball with your non-dominant heel. At the same time, bring your dominant foot forward to help you land. Do all steps in one quick motion. The ball should pop up over you in a high curve. Keep running forward to recover the ball when it lands.

CHIP

Use this kicking technique to send the ball curving up into the air. As you approach the ball, plant one foot to the side of the ball. Swing your other leg back. A shorter swing will give you more control over the ball. Point your toes and bring your foot under the ball. Scoop the ball up and launch it into the air. The chip is good for passing, getting the ball past opponents, and tricking the goalie.

BENDING KICK

Curve the ball in midair with this expert kick. Approach the ball at an angle. Plant one foot to the side of the ball. Strike the ball with the inside of your other foot. Start at the bottom corner of the ball, and kick up and around it. Be sure to finish with your shoulders pointed in the direction you want the ball to travel. Use the bend to pass around an opponent or for shots on goal.

GLOSSARY

determination (di-tur-muh-NEY-shuhn)—the quality or act of continuing to try do something and not giving up, even though it may be difficult

drill (DRIL)—a repetitive exercise that helps you learn a specific skill

embarrassment (em-BAR-uhss-muhnt)—something or someone that causes you or a group to feel uncomfortable and foolish in front of others

experience (ik-SPIHR-ee-uhnss)—knowledge or skill gained from doing something

frustrations (fruh-STREY-shuhnz)—feelings of anger and annoyance because of something not going as planned or not being able to do something

humiliated (hyoo-MIL-ee-ate-ed)—made to feel ashamed and foolish

instincts (IN-stingktz)—behaviors that you don't have to think about in order to do

legend (LEJ-uhnd)—a person who is famous for doing something very well

retire (ri-TIRE)—to stop doing an activity or working a job, often because of old age

ridiculous (ri-DIK-yuh-luhss)—extremely silly and against common sense

scrimmage (SKRIM-ij)—a practice game between members of the same team

virtues (vir-CHOOZ)—very good qualities or features

READ THEM ALL!

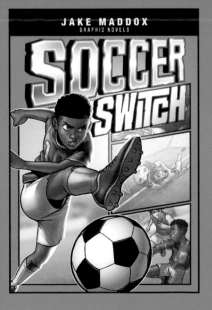

FIND OUT MORE AT
WWW.MYCAPSTONE.COM

ABOUT THE AUTHOR

Brandon Terrell is the author of numerous children's books, including six volumes in the Tony Hawk's 900 Revolution series and several Sports Illustrated Kids Graphic Novels. When not hunched over his laptop writing, Brandon enjoys watching movies, reading, watching and playing baseball, and spending time with his wife and two children in Minnesota.

ABOUT THE ILLUSTRATOR

Aburtov has worked in the comic book industry for more than eleven years. In that time, he has illustrated popular characters such as Wolverine, Iron Man, Blade, and the Punisher. Recently, Aburtov started his own illustration studio called Graphikslava. He lives in Monterrey, Mexico, with his daughter, Ilka, and his beloved wife. Aburtov enjoys spending his spare time with family and friends.